JE

For Jack Drake,
my favorite dentist
—I.W.

For Mr. Jon Harris,
who is a good brusher
—A.R.

Text copyright © 2000 by Ian Whybrow
Illustrations copyright © 2000 by Adrian Reynolds

First American edition 2002 published by Orchard Books
This edition first published in Great Britain in 2001 by Gullane Children's Books

Ian Whybrow and Adrian Reynolds assert the moral right to be identified as the author and the
illustrator of this work.

Library of Congress Cataloging-in-Publication Data
Whybrow, Ian.
Sammy and the dinosaurs say "ahhh!" / by Ian Whybrow ; illustrated by Adrian Reynolds.—lst American ed.
p. cm.
Summary: A young boy takes his toy dinosaurs with him to help calm his fears on his first visit to the dentist.
ISBN 0-439-32686-9 (alk. paper)
[1. Dentists—Fiction. 2. Dinosaurs—Fiction. 3. Toys—Fiction.] I. Reynolds, Adrian, ill. II. Title.
PZ7.W6225 San 2002 [E]—dc21 2001-032934

10 9 8 7 6 5 4 3 2 1   02 03 04 05

Printed in Italy

The text of this book is set in 21 point Goudy. The illustrations are watercolor.

Sammy
and the Dinosaurs
Say "Ahhh!"

by IAN WHYBROW

illustrated by ADRIAN REYNOLDS

ORCHARD BOOKS • NEW YORK
An Imprint of Scholastic Inc.

Mom had her coat on,
but Sammy was being slow.
They were going to see
Dr. Drake, the dentist.

Sammy was a little scared.
That was because of Meg
showing him her filling.

Sammy wanted to take his dinosaurs, but they were hiding all over the house. He called out their names.

He said, "Get in the bucket, my Stegosaurus."
And out came Stegosaurus from under
the pillow.

He said, "Get in the bucket, my Triceratops."
And out came Triceratops from inside
the drawer.

One by one, Brontosaurus and Scelidosaurus
and Anchisaurus all came out of their hiding
places and jumped into the bucket.

All except for Tyrannosaurus. He didn't want
to go because he had a lot of teeth.
He thought Dr. Drake might drill them.

Sammy said, "Don't worry, because when we get there
I will press a magic button on my bucket.
And that will make you grow big."

In the waiting room the nurse said,
"Hello, Sammy. Are you a good boy?"
    Sammy said, "I am, but my dinosaurs bite."

Then Dr. Drake called,
"Next, please!"

The nurse took Sammy into Dr. Drake's room.
Sammy wasn't sure about the big chair. He thought
maybe that was where Dr. Drake did the drilling.

"Come and have a ride in my chair," said Dr. Drake.
"It goes up and down."

Sammy didn't want to ride.

"Would one of your dinosaurs like a ride?"
asked Dr. Drake.

Sammy put Tyrannosaurus on the chair.
He whispered to him not to worry,
then he pressed the magic button . . . and
Tyrannosaurus grew *very* big!

"Open wide," said Dr. Drake,
and then he turned around. . . .

"RAAAAAAH!" said Tyrannosaurus.
"Help!" cried Dr. Drake.
And he hid behind the door.
Dr. Drake said, "Sammy, what
should I do?"

Sammy pressed the magic button.
Right away, Tyrannosaurus
went back to being bucket-size.

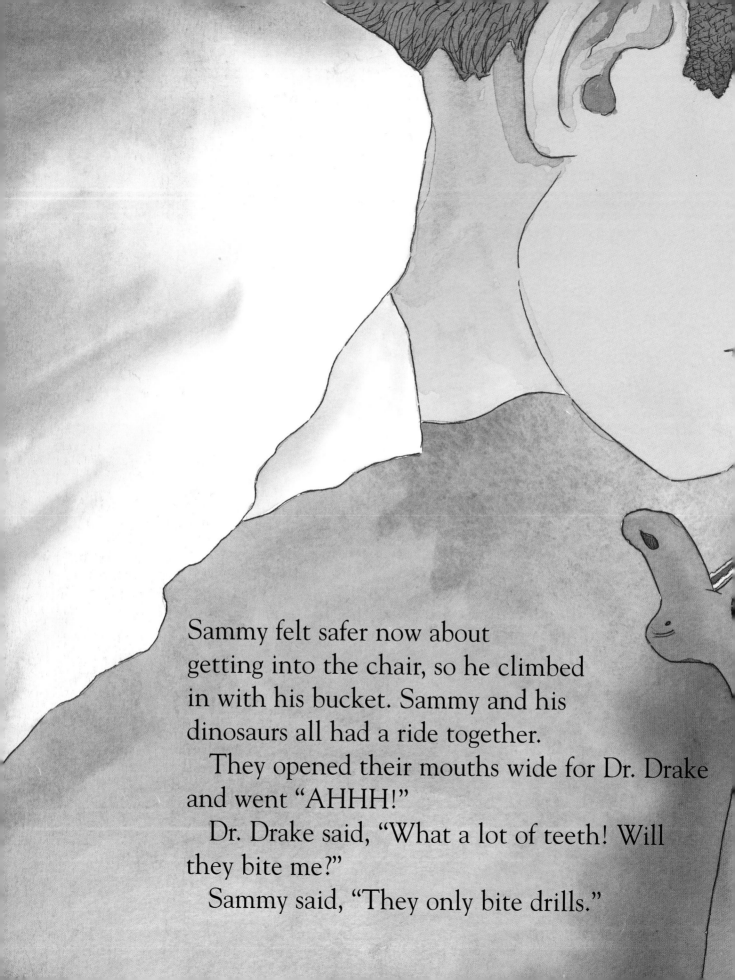

Sammy felt safer now about
getting into the chair, so he climbed
in with his bucket. Sammy and his
dinosaurs all had a ride together.

They opened their mouths wide for Dr. Drake
and went "AHHH!"

Dr. Drake said, "What a lot of teeth! Will
they bite me?"

Sammy said, "They only bite drills."

"You are all good brushers," said Dr. Drake,
"so no drills today—only a look
and a rinse."

All the dinosaurs liked riding in the big chair, and they liked rinsing.

"Another bucket of mouthwash, Joan!" called Dr. Drake.

On the way home, Mom let Sammy choose a book from the library for being so good.

"Let's have a shark book," said Sammy.

"RAAAAH!" said the dinosaurs.
"Sharp teeth! We like sharks!"

Endosaurus.